CREATE YOUR OWN
SUPER-
HERO
STORIES

BARRON'S

First edition for the United States and Canada published in 2011
by Barron's Educational Series, Inc.

First published in Great Britain in 2010 by Buster Books, an imprint of
Michael O'Mara Books Limited, 9 Lion Yard, Tremadoc Road, London SW4, 7NQ

Written by: Liz Scoggins
Illustrated by: Paul Moran
Designed by: Zoe Quayle

All inquiries should be addressed to:
Barron's Educational Series, Inc.
250 Wireless Boulevard
Hauppauge, New York 11788
www.barronseduc.com

Library of Congress Control Number: 2010936552

ISBN: 978-0-7641-4680-0

Date of Manufacture: December 2010
Place of Manufacture: WKT Co. Ltd., Shenzhen, China

Printed in China
9 8 7 6 5 4 3 2 1

SUPERHERO STORIES

Write your name below and fill the page with superheroes.

By ....

Creating Your Stories

It's time to create your own superhero stories—you can add some of the words provided or choose your own, and complete the pictures yourself. When you've finished this book, you will have a collection of stories that is all yours—different from everyone else's.

Missing Pictures

Each page has pictures for you to finish yourself. Let your imagination go wild—it's completely up to you what doodles you do.

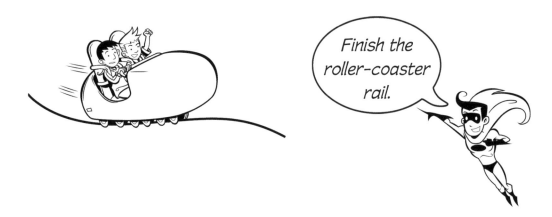

Finish the roller-coaster rail.

Missing Words

In this book, you will find unfinished sentences with empty boxes to fill.

Look at the pictures and decide which words to put in each box. There are no right words or wrong words—it's up to you. If you need some help, on each page there is a selection of words you can choose from.

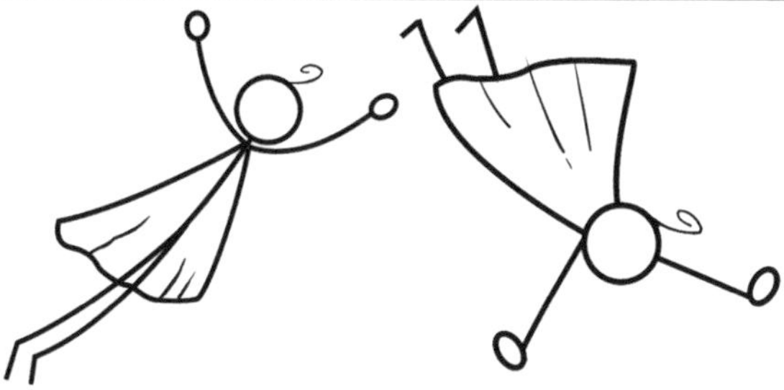

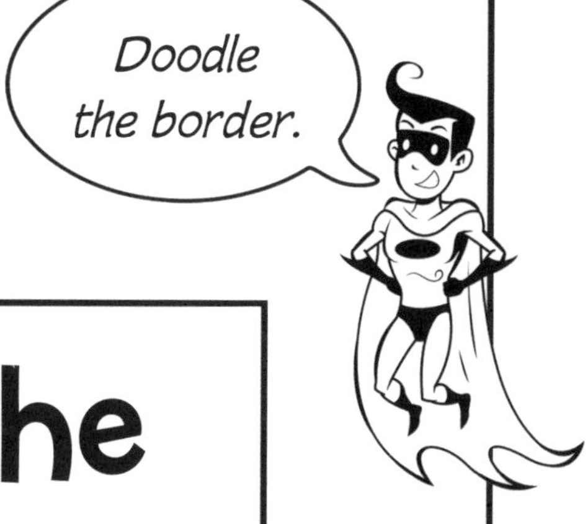
Doodle the border.

Jack to the Rescue

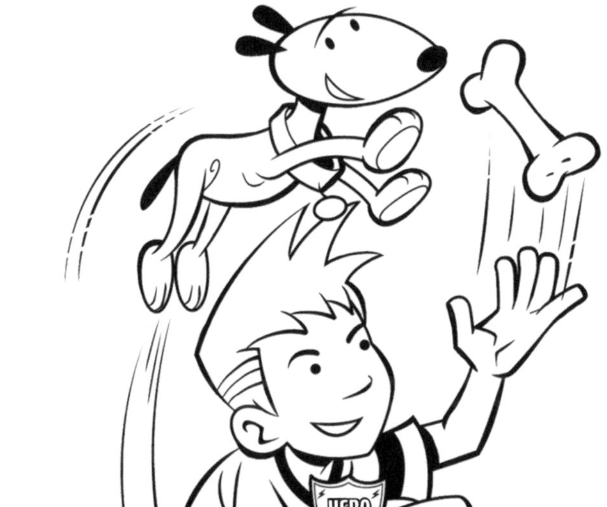
HERO

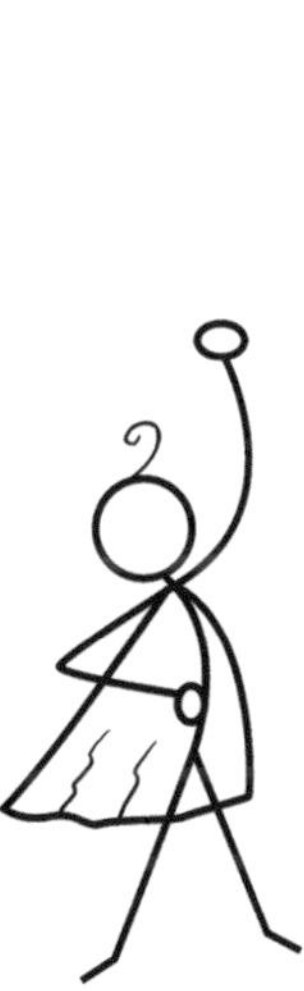

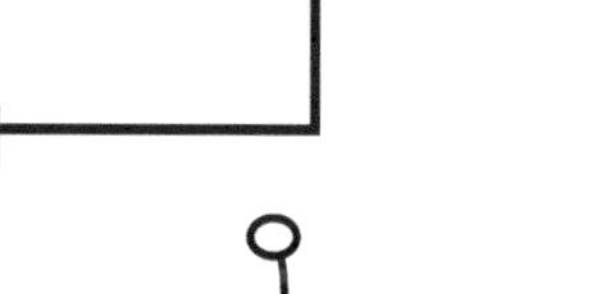

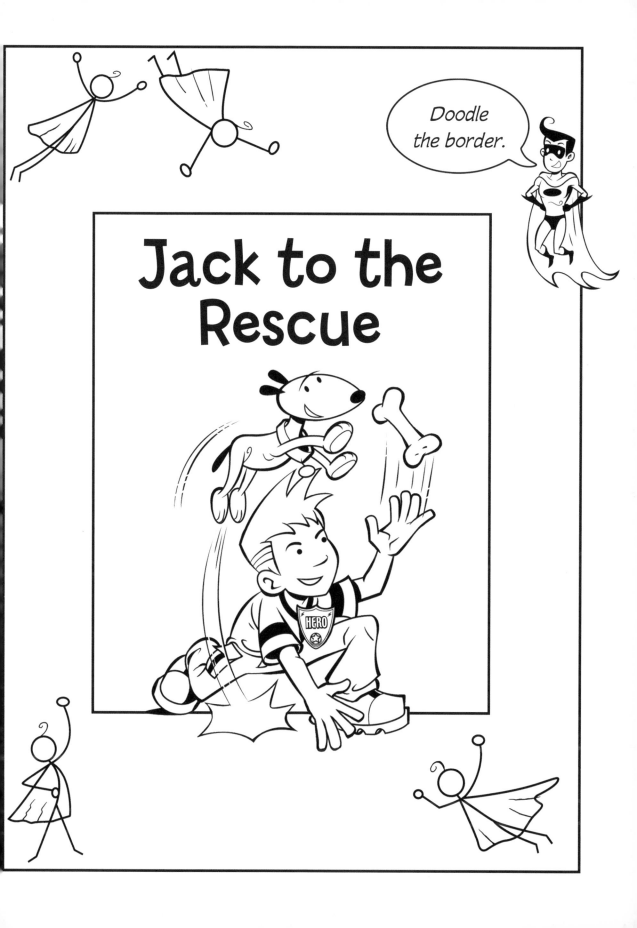

One weekend, Jack was really bored. His dad gave him a box of his old ⬚ to look at.

Fill the box with Dad's things.

Inside the box, Jack found [　　　　　　　　] and [　　　　　　　　] . He also found a badge with the word "Hero" on it.

You could use some of these words or choose your own:

comics   toys   bricks   cars   balls   robots

That night, Jack had a dream. In his dream he was a superhero. He could [_____] really high, and [_____] very fast.

You could use some of these words or choose your own:

jump   bounce   fly   run   swim

Can you doodle a superhero?

The next day, Jack and his best friend Ben went to the _____ . They climbed a tree that was as big as a _____ .

You could use some of these words or choose your own:

park   garden   forest   house   bus   mountain

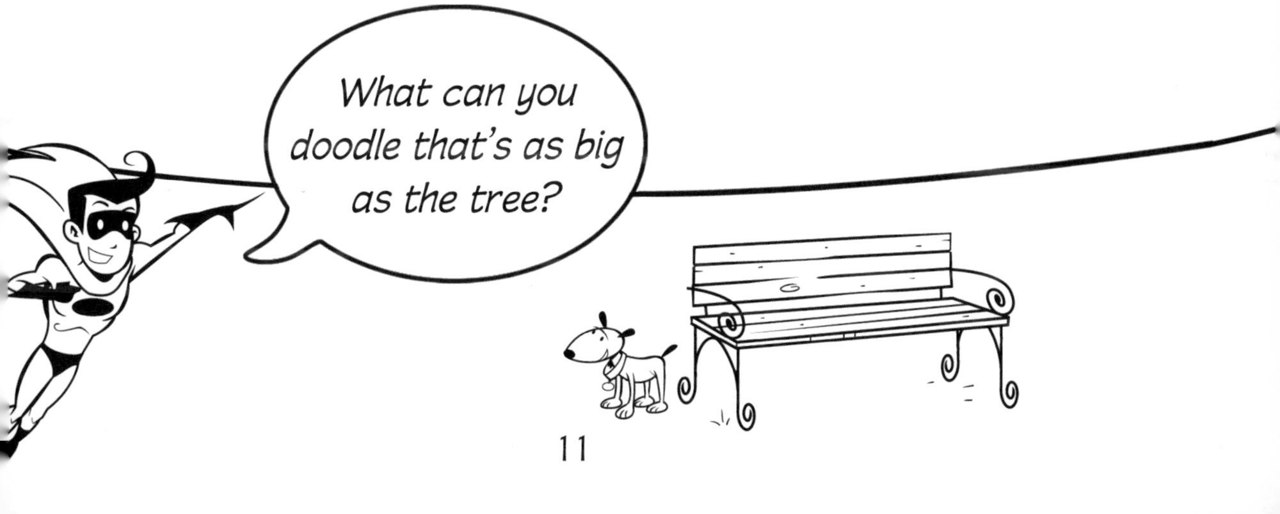
What can you doodle that's as big as the tree?

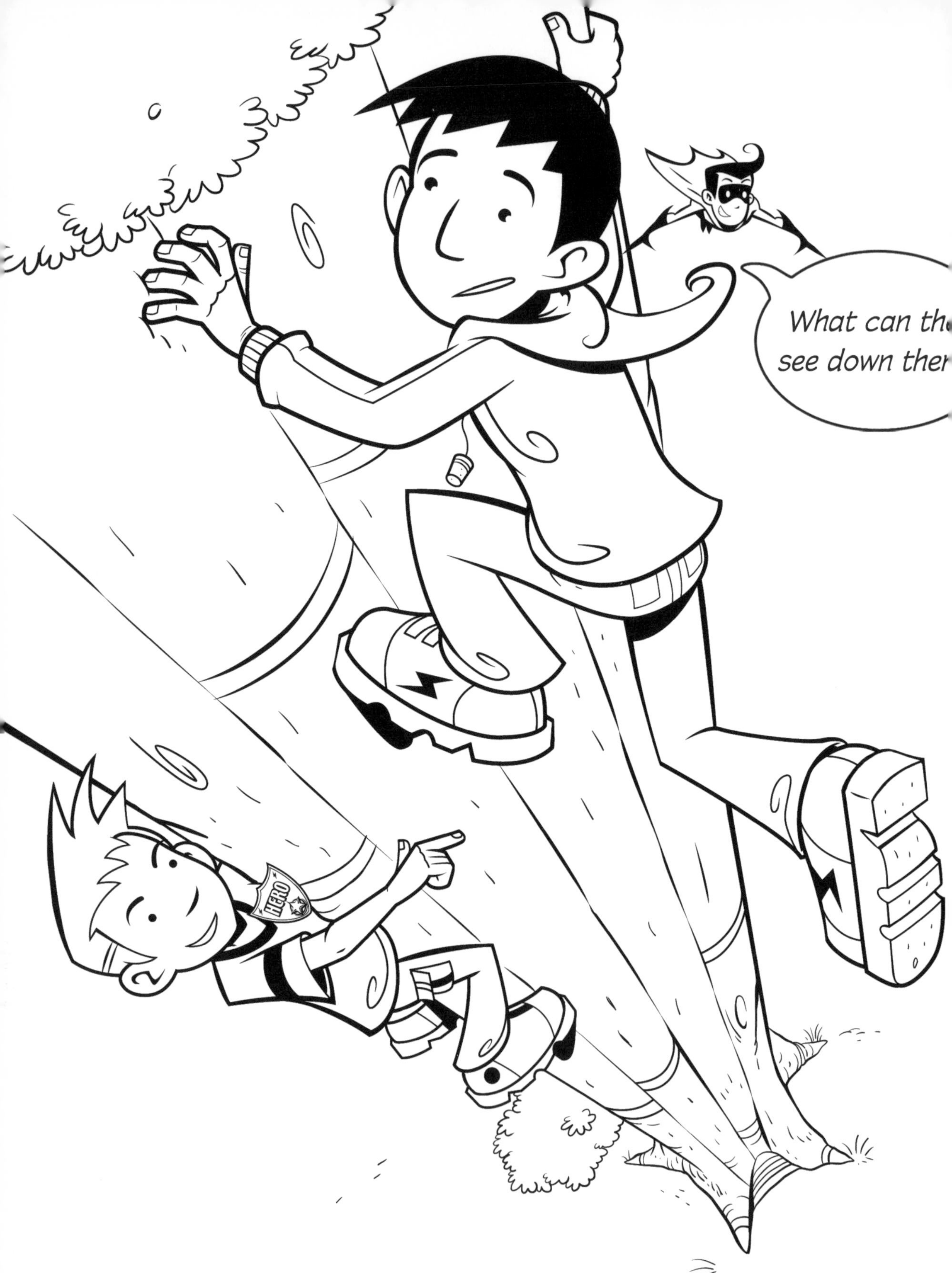

What can th
see down ther

Ben climbed too high. When he looked down he felt

very [   ] . Down below, he could

see a [   ] and some very small

[   ] .

You could use some of these words or choose your own:

sick   afraid   bike   pond   people   animals

Jack suddenly realized he could fly to the top of the tree! He lifted Ben _____ from the branch and carried him _____ to the ground. Maybe Jack really was a superhero?

Can you draw Ben?

You could use some of these words or choose your own:

carefully　　　gently　　　slowly　　　quickly

Doodle the border.

Jack and Dog at the Park

Jack and Dog decided to [ ] in the park. It was a very [ ] day.

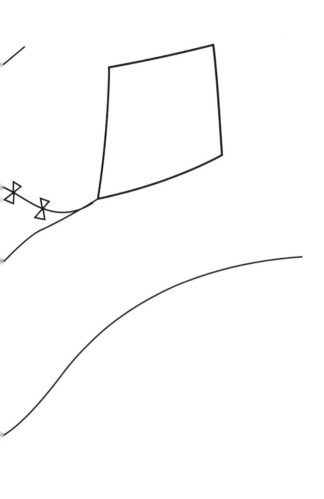

Fill the sky with kites.

You could use some of these words or choose your own:

walk   run   play   sunny   cloudy   windy

When they got to the swings, Jack and Dog could

[   ] a little girl. She started to

[   ] . Jack stopped and asked her

what was wrong.

You could use some of these words or choose your own:

see   hear   cry   shout

Doodle more swings and a slide, too.

"I've lost my big sister!" said the little girl. So Jack told her to wait there [_____] with Dog and rushed off out of sight.

You could use some of these words or choose your own:

patiently   calmly   quietly   tree   bush   fence

Jack hid behind a [_____] , and when no one was looking, he jumped into the sky.

Jack began to [blank] above the park, to [blank] the little girl's older sister. He soon saw her by the [blank] .

You could use some of these words or choose your own:

fly   hover   find   spot   pond   tree

Jack went to [   ] the girl where her little sister was. She was so [   ] that she got everyone an ice cream!

Doodle four amazing ice creams.

You could use some of these words or choose your own:

tell   show   happy   relieved   pleased

Adventure
at the Fair

*Doodle
the border.*

The fair was coming to town, and Jack and Ben were very

[   ]. The two boys talked non-stop

about which rides they would go on the next day.

You could use some of these words or choose your own:

excited   bored   nervous   impatient

Design a poster for the fair.

Ben got up early the next morning and looked out of the window. The sky was dark and [   ] .

You could use some of these words or choose your own:

cloudy   stormy   disappointed   upset   sad

The boys were very [   ].
The storm would spoil the fair. Jack decided to do
something about it.

Jack looked up at the clouds. He took a deep breath and began to blow as hard as he could.

At first, nothing happened, but then the clouds started to [   ] . Jack blew harder and the sky got [   ] again.

You could use some of these words or choose your own:

move   vanish   brighter   sunnier

Ben waited and waited outside the fair. He began to

[   ] that he would have to go in

without Jack.

You could use some of these words or choose your own:

worry   think   town   fair   park

Jack reappeared at Ben's side as the sun shone down on the [   ] . "Come on," said Jack. "We'll miss all the fun!"

Fill the fairground with people.

Jack and Ben ran [ ] to the roller coaster. It looked [ ] .

Finish the roller-coaster rail.

You could use some of these words or choose your own:

quickly   excitedly   fun   terrifying   fantastic

A Visit to Granny's House

Doodle the border.

Jack and Dog were going to spend the weekend at Granny's. She lived in the [   ] .

You could use some of these words or choose your own:

town   country   apples   sandwiches

Jack and Dog packed [   ] to eat on the train.

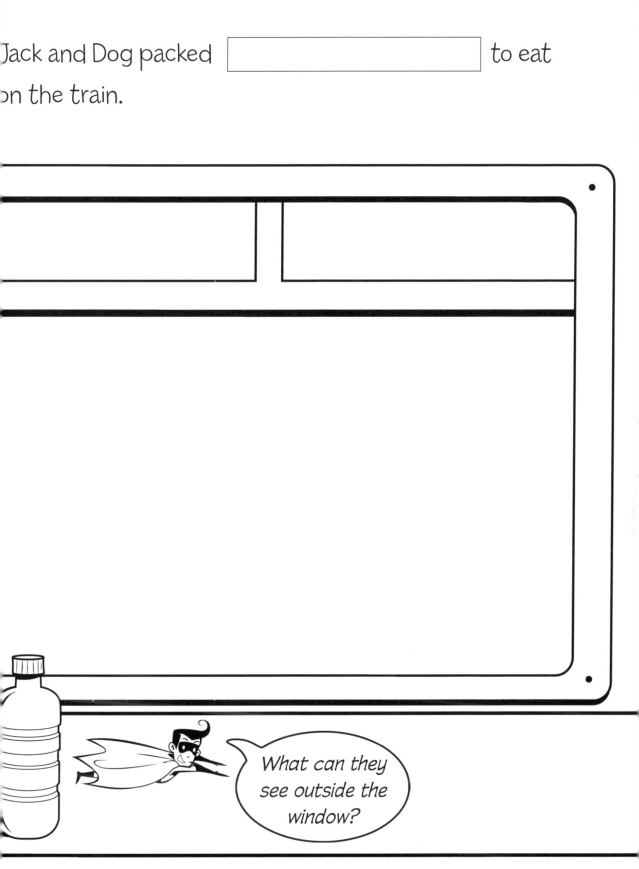

What can they see outside the window?

Granny met Jack and Dog at the station. She gave Jack a [   ] , and patted Dog's head.

Doodle the train on the tracks.

You could use some of these words or choose your own:

kiss   hug   chicken   peas   eggs   salad

Granny cooked Jack's favorite dinner. They had

[   ] and [   ] .

What is on
Jack's plate?

After dinner, Jack and Dog went to bed, while Granny made a [_____] cup of tea. It had been a very long day.

Suddenly, Granny heard a ⬚⬚⬚⬚⬚⬚⬚⬚⬚ .

She ran up the stairs ⬚⬚⬚⬚⬚⬚⬚⬚ to see

what had happened.

You could use some of these words or choose your own:

hot   lovely   bark   crash   quickly   quietly

To Granny's surprise Jack had started to

[   ] above his bed in his sleep!

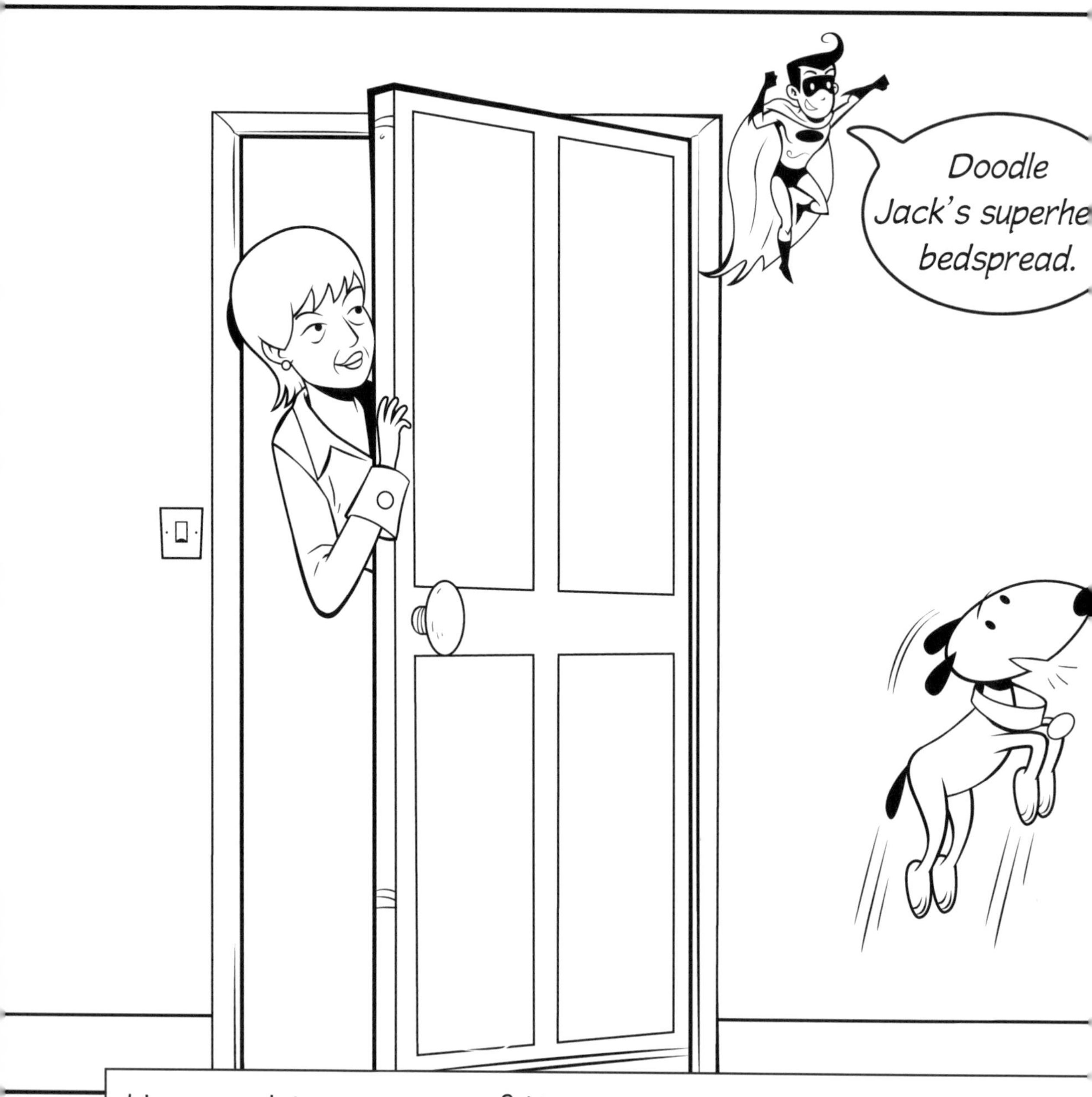
Doodle
Jack's superhe
bedspread.

You could use some of these words or choose your own:

hover   fly   room   door

She smiled and tiptoed quietly out of the

_____ .

At breakfast the next morning, Granny shut her eyes and began to _____ . To Jack's amazement the food flew up from the table! "Granny," Jack said, "you're just like me!"

Can you draw their breakfast hovering?

You could use some of these words or choose your own:

frown   concentrate   smile

Doodle
the border.

Jack's Underwater Adventure

In the [   ] , Jack's parents took him and Dog to a cottage at the beach.

Doodle their footprints.

You could use some of these words or choose your own:

summer   spring   golden   wet

On the first morning, Jack and Dog went for a walk along the [   ] sand.

Dog wanted to [＿＿＿＿＿＿＿＿] ahead, chasing seagulls. This made them very upset. One of the seagulls swooped down and managed to [＿＿＿＿＿＿＿＿] the key to the cottage from Jack's fingers.

You could use some of these words or choose your own:

race   run   pluck   grab   naughty   bad

Jack leaped into the air, following the seagull. The
_____ seagull flew out over the water
and dropped the key into the waves.

Oh no! They couldn't get inside the cottage without the key. So Jack decided to _____ into the waves after it.

Complete the underwater scene.

You could use some of these words or choose your own:

plunge   dive   sand   seaweed   shipwreck   shells

He hunted in the [_____] and the [_____] for a long time. To Jack's surprise, he discovered that he did not need to go back up for air. He could breathe under water!

Under the water Jack could see lots of brightly patterned fish, a [_____] , an eel, a starfish and even a [_____] .

Draw the lost key.

You could use some of these words or choose your own:

lobster   shark   crab   mermaid   quickly   excitedly

As soon as Jack spotted the key he grabbed it and swam [_____] to the surface.

Can you doodle the splashes?

Jack decided to [_____] Dog back up the beach. They both shook themselves to dry out, and Jack [_____] gave back the key.

Doodle the cottage.

You could use some of these words or choose your own:

race   chase   beat   proudly   happily

Doodle
the border.

Dog Goes Missing

After school one day, Jack wanted to take Dog to the

[   ] , but he could not find him.

Jack called out, "Dog!" Dog didn't come. Where was he?

What can Jack see through the door?

You could use some of these words or choose your own:

park   woods   kitchen   bedroom   garage

Jack went to look in the [   ] , but before he opened the door he realized he could see straight through it! "X-ray vision," said Jack. "Great!"

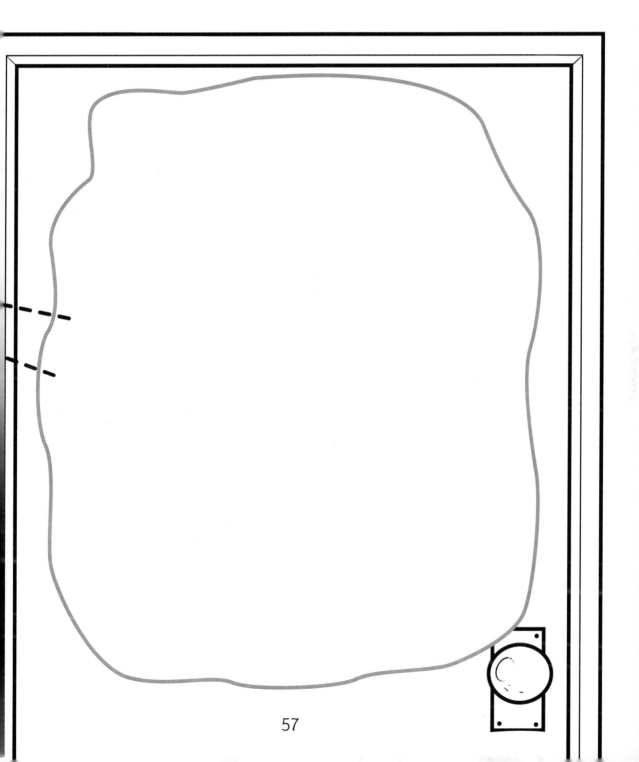

With his new power, Jack searched the whole house. Outside, Dog had dug a big [   ]. He was so far down that only Jack's X-ray eyes could see him.

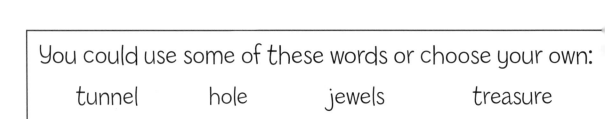

You could use some of these words or choose your own:

tunnel   hole   jewels   treasure

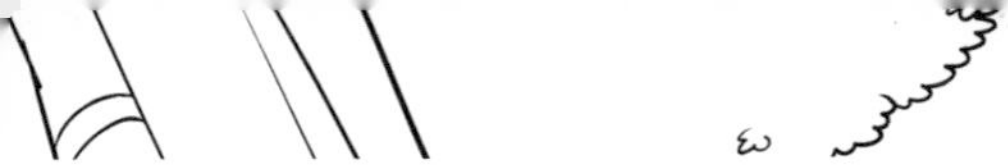

Next to Dog under the ground, Jack spotted something shiny. Dog had found some ________________ !

"Well done, Dog," yelled Jack.

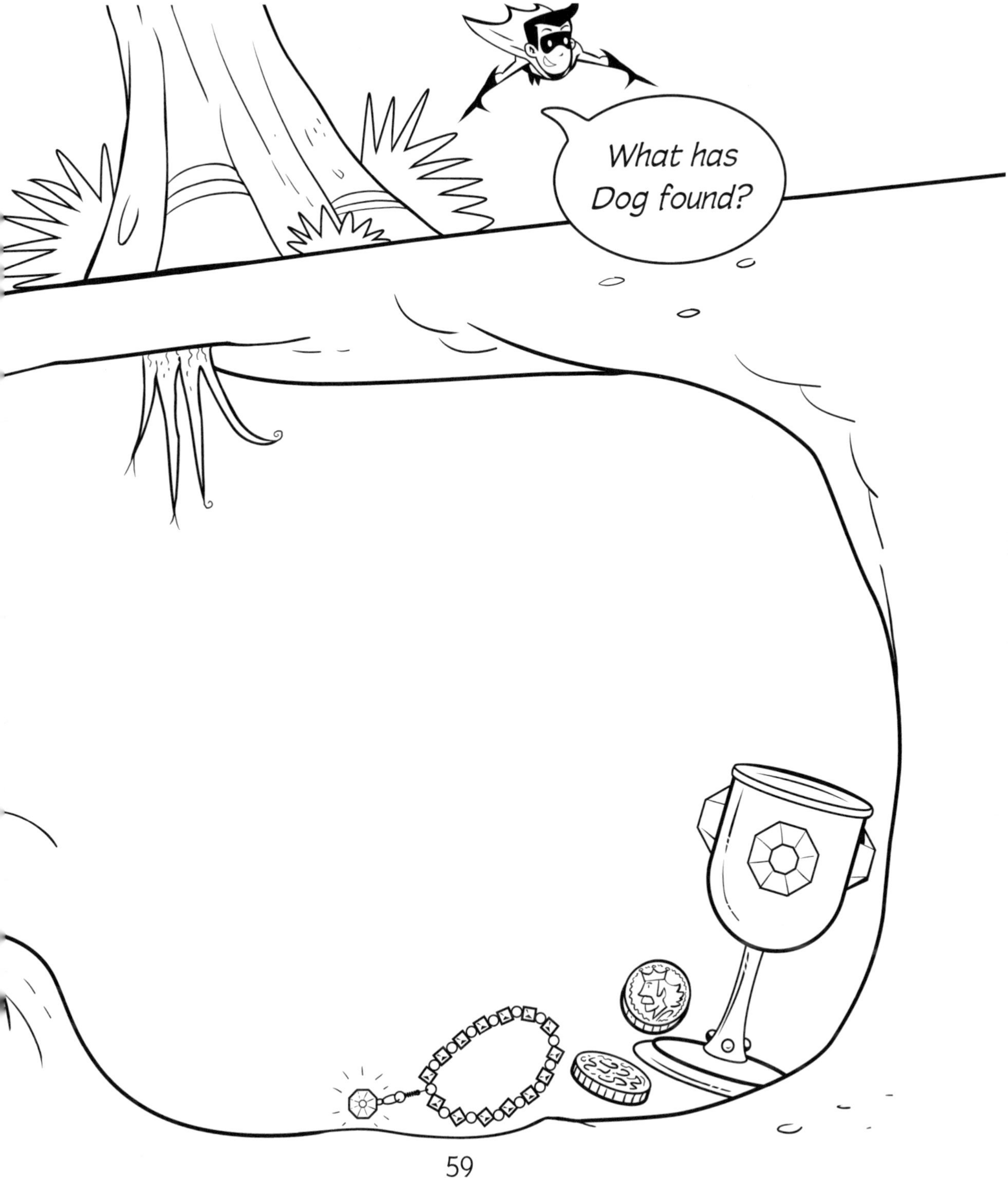
What has Dog found?

Everyone was so [_____] with Jack. The local newspaper sent a reporter to interview them both.

LOCAL HERO FINDS HIDDEN TREASURE

You could use some of these words or choose your own:

impressed   pleased   buy   get

Jack and Dog were in the newspaper the next week.

Jack's parents decided to ⬚

twenty copies and sent one to Granny at once.

Doodle Jack and Dog's picture.

Granny was so thrilled to [   ] Jack's amazing story in the newspaper that she sent him a [   ] gift: his own superhero costume.

Doodle Jack's costume.

You could use some of these words or choose your own:

see   read   wonderful   special

The End

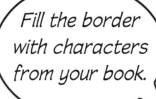

Fill the border with characters from your book.

HOURS OF DOODLING FUN FOR KIDS

Kids love to doodle—and these books inspire young doodle experts to stretch their imaginations and have fun. They're packed with comical cartoon-style illustrations, but every picture has important missing details. It's up to young artists to pick up a pencil or marker pen and make each picture complete in any way that they choose. The funnier, the better! Here are three lively titles that promise kids many hours of imaginative, laugh-provoking entertainment. (Ages 7 and older)

Zoodles!

Oodles of Animal Pictures to Finish!

Illustrated by Peter Coupe
978-0-7641-4501-8, Paperback, 176 pp.
$8.99, Can$10.99

Doodle Mania

Oodles of Fun Pictures to Finish!

Illustrated by Peter Coupe
978-0-7641-4500-1, Paperback, 176 pp.
$8.99, Can$10.99

Doodle Bug

Catch the Doodle Bug!

978-0-7641-6351-7, Hardcover w/spiral binding, 192 pp.
$9.99, Can$11.99

 To order ————
Available at your local book store
or visit **www.barronseduc.com**

(#203) R9/0

Barron's Educational Series, Inc.
250 Wireless Blvd.
Hauppauge, N.Y. 11788
Order toll-free: 1-800-645-3476

Prices subject to change without notice.

In Canada:
Georgetown Book Warehouse
34 Armstrong Ave.
Georgetown, Ontario L7G 4R9
Canadian orders: 1-800-247-71